A COYOTE SOLSTICE TALE

BY
THOMAS KING

PICTURES BY
GARY CLEMENT

GROUNDWOOD BOOKS
HOUSE OF ANANSI PRESS
TORONTO   BERKELEY

Groundwood Books / House of Anansi Press
110 Spadina Avenue, Suite 801, Toronto, Ontario M5V 2K4
or c/o Publishers Group West
1700 Fourth Street, Berkeley, CA 94710

We acknowledge for their financial support of our publishing
program the Canada Council for the Arts, the Government of Canada
through the Book Publishing Industry Development Program
(BPIDP), and the Ontario Arts Council.

ONTARIO ARTS COUNCIL
CONSEIL DES ARTS DE L'ONTARIO

Library and Archives Canada Cataloguing in Publication
King, Thomas
A Coyote solstice tale / Thomas King ; Gary Clement, illustrator.
ISBN 978-0-88899-929-0
1. Coyote (Legendary character)—Juvenile fiction.
2. Consumption (Economics)—Juvenile fiction. I. Clement, Gary
II. Title.
PS8571.I5298C694 2009   jC813'.54   C2009-901067-4

Design by Michael Solomon
Printed and bound in China

For my mother
on the occasion of her
eighty-fifth birthday
TK

To Gill, Sarah and Ben
GC

The World was a wintry wonder
The snow piled in mounds on the ground

While Coyote was anxiously waiting
For all of his friends to come round.

There's nothing like a feast, said Coyote.

Then out in the heart of the forest
Where the trees block the light of the moon
Came the cadence of somebody prancing
And humming a holiday tune.

It's Beaver and Bear, cried Coyote.
And he rushed to the door arms
outspread.

But there on the porch in the
    moonlight
Was a little girl all dressed in red.

Hello, said the girl, I'm a reindeer.
And she pawed at the snow with
    her toes.
She had sticks in her hair and a
    green teddy bear
And a red rubber ball on her nose.

Good grief, said Coyote quite shaken
For he knew as everyone knows
That people and creatures stopped
    talking
A couple of eons ago.

Hmmm, said Coyote, this could be
    awkward.

I've come to the woods, yawned the
    reindeer
To find friendship and goodwill and peace.
And she curled up in front of the fire
And she wrapped herself up in a fleece.

Good grief, said Coyote quite shaken
For he knew as everyone knows
That people and creatures stopped
    talking
A couple of eons ago.

Hmmm, said Coyote, this could be
    awkward.

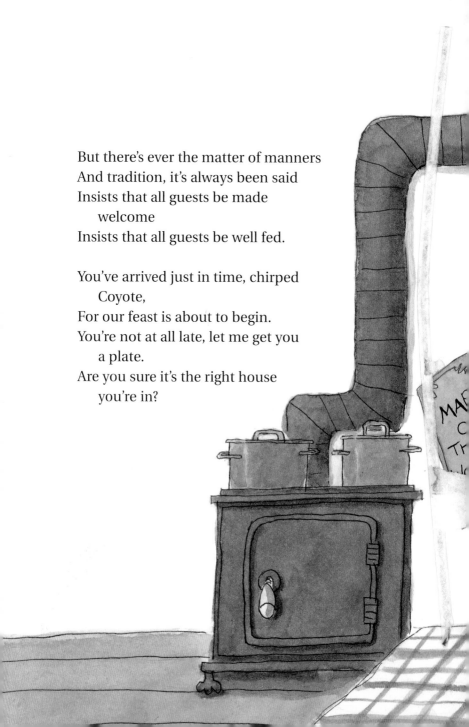

But there's ever the matter of manners
And tradition, it's always been said
Insists that all guests be made
    welcome
Insists that all guests be well fed.

You've arrived just in time, chirped
    Coyote,
For our feast is about to begin.
You're not at all late, let me get you
    a plate.
Are you sure it's the right house
    you're in?

I've come to the woods, yawned the
    reindeer
To find friendship and goodwill and peace.
And she curled up in front of the fire
And she wrapped herself up in a fleece.

Then out on the star-brightened meadow
The ice crystals tickling their feet
Came Beaver and Bear and Otter and Moose
Their bags filled with groceries and treats.

Get in here, said Coyote. You have to see this.

She's probably lost, offered Beaver.
It happens this time of the year.
Let's follow her footprints back through the snow
To see how she got way out here.

So the animals put on their woollies
And Moose set the girl on his back
And they tromped through the dark frosty
    evening
Til they came to the end of her track.

Hey, said Coyote, what happened to all the trees?

And there at the edge of the clear-cut
Set alone 'gainst the western skies
Was an object so bright that it lit up the night
And made everyone cover their eyes.

All the animals stood around squinting
At this sight full of wonder and fear.
It has to be new, stuttered Otter,
For it wasn't here this time last year.

The little girl straightened her antlers
And she jumped down onto the snow.
Oh, that's just the mall, she said,
    fixing her nose.
It's no place that you want to go.

COMPUTERS CAMERAS STUFF GAMES TV

A mall, said the animals. What's a mall?

So down the steep slope they tobogganed
Sliding right through the packed parking lot
Then in through the doors onto faux-marble
  floors
Where the lights were dynamic and hot.

The noise was completely unnerving
The music a pain to the ear.
All the people were bumping and pushing
Attempting to find a cashier.

The animals huddled together
As rough herds of humans rushed by
Their arms filled with brightly wrapped boxes
And murderous looks in their eyes

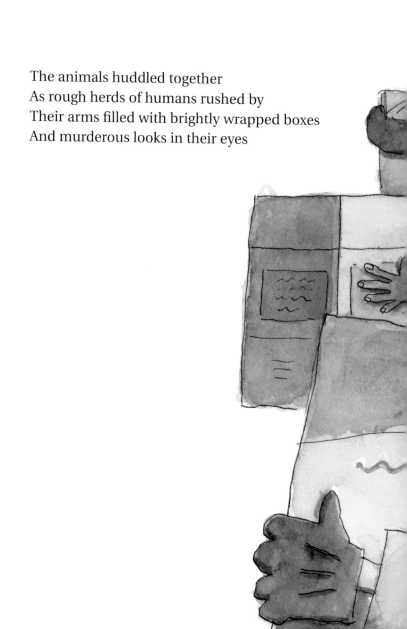

So this is what humans do, said Coyote.

And before anybody could stop him
Coyote was out on the floor
Loading every new thing in his basket
As he scampered and skipped through
        the store.

Here's a plasma-screen TV for Otter
And a digital wristwatch for Bear
Four volumes of Proust for my good
    friend the Moose
And for Beaver a vibrating chair.

So up to the checkout he swaggered.
Who knew shopping could be such a thrill?
Then the sales woman tallied his presents
And cheerfully passed him the bill.

You've made some exceptional choices,
    she said,
And excess is truly the key.
Will you purchase these items with credit
    or cash
Or buy them on time, interest free?

Purchase? said Coyote.

The stars overhead were
    resplendent
When Coyote slouched out of the
    mall.
I'm sorry you all had to see that,
Said the girl with the red rubber
    ball.

That's why I pretend I'm a reindeer
And put these two sticks in my hair.
I'd much rather live in a generous
    world
Where everyone knows how to
    share.

But my parents are probably worried
So I ought to return straight aways.
But perhaps I could visit next season
And stay for a couple of days.

Sure, said Coyote, reindeer are always
welcome at my place.

The world was a wintry wonder
With the rumors of light in the east
As the animals strolled to Coyote's
To continue their seasonal feast.

All this walking has made me quite hungry
All that shopping has left me quite numb
I may have to rest, said Coyote,
And wait for refreshments to come.

So Otter and Moose made corn chowder
And Beaver and Bear baked the bread
While Coyote lay there in his
    comfortable chair
With a pillow tucked under his head.

And after the eating and drinking
After all of the stories were told
After most of the mess had been tidied…

Everybody went out in the cold
To sing as the light filled the heavens
To welcome a splendid new day
And offer a prayer for clean water and air
Then they parted, and went their own way.

And Coyote…
Well, he sat on the porch in his rocker
And he rocked as he tried to recall
If goodwill and peace could be purchased
For credit or cash at the mall.